D1314823

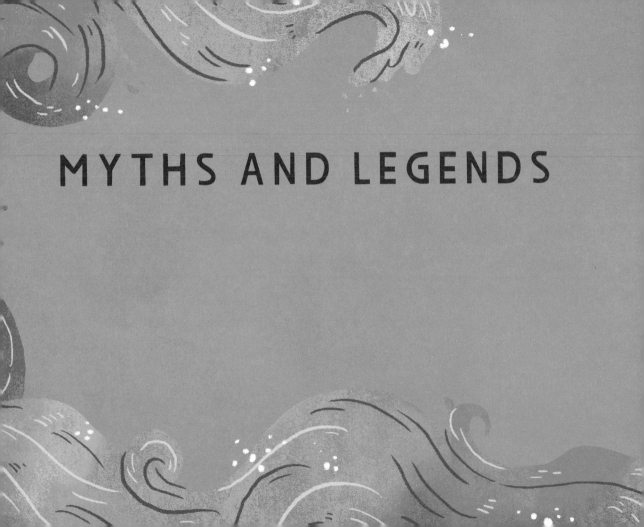

MYTHS AND LEGENDS

360 DEGREES, an imprint of Tiger Tales
5 River Road, Suite 128, Wilton, CT 06897
Published in the United States 2017
Originally published in Great Britain 2017
by Little Tiger Press
Text copyright © 2017 Sandra Lawrence
Illustrations copyright © 2017 Emma Trithart
ISBN-13: 978-1-944530-11-2
ISBN-10: 1-944530-11-8
Printed in China
CPB/1800/0658/0217
10 9 8 7 6 5 4 3 2 1

For more insight and activities, visit us at www.tigertalesbooks.com

MYTHS AND LEGENDS

by Sandra Lawrence • Illustrated by Emma Trithart

INTRODUCTION

People have always told stories. Often, no one can remember where they came from (or even if they are true!), but they're such good fun that we keep telling them anyway.

Myths are stories people used to tell to explain things they didn't understand about their history, nature, or the world around them. Legends may once have been based on truth, but as they have been told over and over again, with each storyteller adding his or her own twist, they have become fabulous fantasies instead.

This book explores a few such tales from different societies and cultures. Welcome to the wonderful world of myths and legends....

CONTENTS

The Ancient Greek gods
lived on Mount Olympus.

GODS AND HEROES

In some cultures, there are many gods in the same group or "pantheon," and like some human families, these gods argue and fight with each other all the time! They play with humans like toys and can be very unpredictable, turning from good to evil within moments.

Heroes are mortals who perform incredible deeds. They might save lives, fight magnificent battles, or hideous beasts, or set out on long journeys to distant lands in search of treasure, land, or fame. Sometimes they are sent on a quest by one god just to spite another!

GOOD GODS

Gods in the old tales are like people: very few of them are all good or all bad. You just don't want to meet a good god having a bad day!

Thor, the Norse god of thunder, is not the brightest, and he's always falling for tricks, but he is incredibly loyal. He bravely defends Asgard, the realm of the gods, and will fight against any threat to his friends and family.

Thor,
Norse

Athena,
Ancient Greek

Vishnu,
Hindu

Of course, some gods are *very* good. Hailing from western Europe, Brigid is the Celtic goddess of poetry, healing, and fire. She was so good that when the Christians came to Ireland, they adopted her and made Brigid a saint!

The feathered serpent god, Quetzalcoatl, from Aztec mythology, is not just the god of creation, wind, and farming—he also gave humans chocolate!

Brigid, Celtic

Quetzalcoatl, Aztec

HOLY TECHNOLOGY!

Many gods use magical tools or weapons to channel their power.

Several gods throw thunderbolts when they're angry. Zeus, king of the Ancient Greek gods, uses thunder and lightning to strike his enemies.

The Dagda is the Irish god of life, death, and feasting. His magic cauldron never runs empty. His club is able to kill nine men with one blow, but also return people to life.

The Greek god Hermes, known as Mercury in Roman mythology, carries a staff called a caduceus. It was used by the messenger of the gods to bring about peace or slumber.

Odin's magical spear has its own name: Gungnir, meaning "swaying one." Made by the dwarfs, Gungnir is perfectly balanced so it will hit any target, no matter who throws it.

WE COULD BE HEROES

A hero is someone of enormous strength and/or bravery. In mythology, heroes perform great feats of daring, usually with the help of the gods.

The legendary outlaw Robin Hood lived in Sherwood Forest, England. In folktales he fights against injustice, often stealing from the rich to redistribute the country's wealth to the poor.

Sun Wukong is a reformed Chinese demon. Calling himself the "Monkey King," he was imprisoned for five centuries by the Buddha for bad behavior. When released, he was sent to protect a pilgrim on a long journey, where he proved that he was a hero after all.

Finn MacCool is a legendary Irish hunter-warrior, strong and wise and often portrayed as a magical giant. Some legends claim that MacCool created the Giant's Causeway in Ireland.

Japanese legend Kintarō was super-strong, even as a child. He was brought up in the mountains by a forest witch, and there are many tales of his childhood battles with monsters and demons.

HERACLES: WHEN THE GOING GETS TOUGH...

Greek hero Heracles was the son of Zeus and Alcmene, a mortal woman. As a demi-god, Heracles became a legend when he completed the following 12 almost-impossible tasks, or labors, for King Eurystheus:

1) Kill the Nemean Lion, whose fur couldn't be pierced by a mortal.

2) Destroy the multi-headed serpent, Hydra.

3) Catch the golden Ceryneian Hind.

4) Capture the raging Erymanthian Boar.

5) Clean out King Augeas' stables.

6) Kill the man-eating Stymphalian birds.

7) Capture the rampaging Cretan Bull.

8) Steal Diomedes' man-eating horses.

9) Take the belt of the Amazon queen Hippolyte.

10) Steal the giant Geryon's cattle.

11) Steal apples from Hesperides' garden.

12) Capture Cerberus, the three-headed guard dog of the underworld.

KING ARTHUR: THE ONCE AND FUTURE KING

Nobody knows if Arthur, the legendary king of the Britons, ever existed, but there are numerous tales about Arthur and his knights of the Round Table fighting terrible foes, both magical and human.

As a young man, Arthur pulled an immovable sword from a stone, proving he was the rightful king of England. Some say this was his magical sword Excalibur, but other accounts say the Lady of the Lake appeared from the lake depths to offer Arthur Excalibur after he'd been crowned.

The legend goes on to say that Arthur never really died but instead lies asleep in a place called Avalon, waiting for when Britain needs him most.

THESEUS: THE HIGHLY—STRUNG HERO

King Minos of Crete had a problem: a man-eating beast with the body of a man and the head of a bull, known as the Minotaur. Minos locked the Minotaur in a labyrinth and demanded that his neighbor, King Aegeus, send seven young men and seven young women each year to feed to the monster.

One year, King Aegeus's son, Theseus, decided enough was enough and joined the sacrifices in order to kill the Minotaur and end the annual bloodshed.

On arriving in Crete, Theseus met King Minos's daughter, Ariadne. She wanted to leave her kingdom, and in exchange for safe passage, gave Theseus a ball of string so he could find his way out of the impossible maze.

When he entered the labyrinth, Theseus found and killed the monster and led the other sacrifices back to safety using Ariadne's thread. Returning a hero, he kept his word and took Princess Ariadne away with him.

TRICKSTERS: NOW YOU SEE THEM...

Tricksters appear in many mythologies, and these cunning characters love to cause a little chaos. No one knows what they will do next—it could be nice or nasty, but it will always be interesting!

Spider-god Anansi appears in many African and Caribbean folktales. Though a trickster, he is generally a good and wise character, using his cunning against enemies who are stronger than he. Stories of Anansi are supposed to give humans hope that they can overcome bad situations, too.

The Norse god Loki is always tricking someone into something with his sweet-talking ways. He is a shapeshifter, turning into different animals in different stories—in one tale he even appears in the guise of an old woman! He fell out of favor with the other gods after arranging the death of the happy god Baldr, whom everyone loved, and was imprisoned. It is said that one day Loki will break free to face the Norse gods in one final battle.

Baba Yaga, Russian

Baron Samedi,
Haitian

Medusa,
Ancient Greek

Set,
Egyptian

6.2"
6.0"
5.10"
5.8"
5.6"
5.4"

22

MWAHAHAHA... IT'S THE BAD GUYS!

Very few baddies in folklore are all evil. The witch Baba Yaga, for example, rides in a flying stone bowl and lives in a hut surrounded by skulls. She will try to eat passers-by, but for those who ask nicely, she will tell the truth.

Baron Samedi may look stylish in his top hat and tails, but this Caribbean spirit of death is far from friendly. Lurking on the crossroad between life and death, he waits to dig your grave. But on the plus side, he will make sure you don't turn into a zombie!

Gorgon Medusa can famously turn a man to stone with just one look, and Egyptian bad guy Set is not only incredibly strong, but he is also the god of chaos and destruction—make sure you don't get on his bad side!

NASTY MYTHOLOGICAL BEASTS

The Scottish Kelpie is a water spirit in the shape of a horse that carries children away. It can change into human form, so if you think someone might be a Kelpie, look at his or her hair—it will be full of water reeds.

According to German folklore, the shape-changing Alp may look funny in its magic hat, but beware! This nasty beast sits on the chests of sleepers until they wake up in a breathless terror.

The Greek Chimera is a terrifying mix of a lion's head and body, a serpent's head tail, and an extra goat's head. When Bellerophon was told to kill the beast, he prayed to Athena, who helped him capture the winged horse Pegasus. Riding Pegasus, Bellerophon was able to attack both heads at once.

Mizuchi are water spirits in the form of wingless dragons. They are found at the forks of rivers. Japanese legend tells of one emperor sending human sacrifices to the Mizuchi after angering them by building a dam.

GOOD TRIUMPHS OVER EVIL: HOORAY!

The Hindu demon-king Mahishasura thought he was invincible because he could only be killed by a woman and didn't believe a girl would be capable of such a feat. He became arrogant and began a reign of terror over both humans and gods.

In response, the great gods Brahma, Vishnu, and Shiva joined forces to create Durga, a many-armed, fearsome female warrior. Upon hearing this, Mahishasura and his demons attacked. He changed into many savage beasts, but Durga, filled with the good of the world, fought back, and finally chopped off his head.

MINI STORIES: GODS AND HEROES

The giant Thrym stole Thor's hammer from Asgard and would only return it if he could marry the goddess Freya. When she refused, Thor dressed up in a wedding gown to trick the giant! As Thrym removed his new wife's veil, he discovered the bearded Norse god, who proceeded to slay the giant and reclaim his hammer.

When Hindu god Shiva came home, his son, Ganesha, refused to let him in, so in a fit of rage, Shiva chopped off his head! Parvati, the boy's mother, was so upset that Shiva was ordered to find his son a new one. He returned with a head from the first animal he saw facing north—a baby elephant!

CREATION MYTHS

The biggest question any of us can ask is where we come from. Even today, people can't agree on how the universe began. But before the age of science, mankind had only imagination to rely on.

Men used all of their creative powers to come up with answers to the mysteries of the universe and all the different life forms in it.
From these ideas came creation myths and legends.

"IN THE BEGINNING..."

There are as many myths about the Native American spirit Sky Woman as there are tribes. Most agree that she fell to Earth from an island in the sky and was helped on her fall by the birds and animals of the Earth. She eventually gave birth to twins, the Good Spirit and the Evil Spirit. Each twin then created the world in perfect balance, making sure there was good and evil present in everything.

According to the Australian indigenous myth, the world was once a dark, flat nothing. The Sun, Moon, stars, and life forms were asleep under the surface. At creation, the eternal ancestors burst through the Earth's crust. First came the Sun, followed by the other spirits, who lived together in Dreamtime, creating landscapes and creatures as they traveled.

The Ancient Egyptians believed that the god Atum (though in later Egyptian mythology it was considered to be Ra) made a son and a daughter, Shu (air) and Tefnut (water). Together Shu and Tefnut formed Geb and Nut, the Earth and the sky. Geb and Nut had four children, who were the gods and goddesses of the forces of life: Fertility, Motherhood, Chaos, and Death.

IT'S A GOD-EAT-GOD WORLD

The Ancient Greeks believed that in the beginning, only Chaos existed. From Chaos came Gaea, and the Earth was born. Gaea gave birth to Uranus, the sky, who surrounded her, and between them they created the 12 Titans.

Upon hearing a prophecy that he would be killed by one of his children, the king Titan, Kronos, swallowed his children as soon as they were born.

His wife, Rhea, was furious and in an act of rebellion she hid her last son, Zeus, from her husband, giving Kronos a stone to eat instead.

Zeus later returned to Mount Olympus disguised as a cupbearer. He gave a potion to the unsuspecting Kronos, making the king violently sick. His other children, the pantheon of Greek gods (below), were finally set free.

Hestia

Poseidon

Zeus

Hera

Demeter

Hades

THE TREE OF LIFE

Many cultures, from China and Russia to the Middle East and South America, have the Tree of Life at the center of their mythology. They are different in detail but have very similar features. The roots represent the underworld, the trunk and branches are the Earth, and the green leaves and twigs at the top represent the realm of the gods.

In Norse mythology, Yggdrasil is an enormous ash tree that grows through the three flat discs that make up the world. Its roots are constantly being chewed by a dragon named Nidhogg, who sends insulting messages to an eagle living in the top branches via Ratatoskr, a squirrel who runs up and down the trunk.

MINI STORIES: MORE BEGINNINGS

God Mbombo of the Kuba kingdom, Africa, was alone in a great sea. Suddenly he was violently sick, expelling the Sun, the Moon, and the stars! The heat from the Sun evaporated the water, making land. Mbombo then vomited once more to produce animals and people.

Hindu mythology tells of a giant turtle, named Akupāra, carrying the world, borne by elephants, on his back. But he's not alone! The Chinese and Native Americans also have stories of a cosmic turtle holding up the heavens.

MYTHOLOGY AND THE NATURAL WORLD

Just as stories were made to explain the origins of the world, man also attributed inexplicable things in nature to the workings of the gods. There are gods responsible for mountains, deserts, wind, and rain, and in many cultures, the gods for each natural phenomenon had to be kept happy. If people did something to anger them, they would exact terrible revenge....

SOLAR FLAIR

To our ancestors, the Sun represented not just warmth and light but also health for their animals and growth for their crops. In several mythologies, it was a god or gods who moved the Sun across the sky during the course of a day. Here are a few examples of those daily deities.

The Egyptian Sun god, Ra, transported the flaming orb in two sky-ships called solar barques, one for day (called Madjet), the other for night (called Semektet). The serpent Apophis, god of chaos, always tried to stop Ra, but every morning Ra overcame him, and the Sun rose again.

The Greeks had a similar idea but Helios, a handsome Titan, drove the Sun across the sky in a golden chariot pulled by four fire-spitting horses named Pyrois, Aeos, Aethon, and Phlegon.

But poor Tsohanoai, the Sun god of the Navajo Native Americans, was given no transport at all! It was believed that he would trudge across the sky with the Sun on his back, and at the end of the day he would hang it on a peg, ready for the journey again the next morning.

SEASONAL TALES

The Ancient Greeks explained the changing of the seasons with the story of the god of the underworld, Hades, kidnapping the beautiful Persephone.

Persephone's mother, Demeter, goddess of the harvest, searched for nine days for her lost daughter before she realized what had happened. She begged Hades to return her daughter to the sunlit lands. Hades refused, saying that, as Persephone had eaten four pomegranate seeds of the underworld, she was bound to his kingdom and had to spend her time there.

Eventually, a deal was reached, and Persephone was allowed to return to Earth for eight months of the year, bringing with her new life and the spring. For the other four months, she returns to live underground with Hades, and winter stalks the land above.

THUNDER AND LIGHTNING

The crashes and flashes of violent storms terrified our ancestors. But to each culture, the answer to the dramatic weather was obvious....

————

The Lightning Bird is a mythological creature of South Africa that can summon thunder and lightning by beating its wings and striking its talons.

————

In Chinese mythology, Dian Mu is the Mother of Lightning and produces lightning by flashing mirrors into the sky. Her husband, Lei Gong, creates thunder with a mallet and drum, punishing evil people with his chisel. Lightning flashes before the thunder so that Lei Gong can make sure he is punishing the right person before he strikes.

A DAZZLING NATURAL LIGHTSHOW

How do you explain something as magical as the aurora borealis?
In Finnish folklore, the Revontulet, or "Fox Fire," is caused by a magical
fox sweeping his tail across the snow, swishing it into the sky.

The Cree Indians believed the colorful lights were the souls of their departed loved ones, while some Inuit tribes said it was the spirits of the dead playing football with a walrus skull!

———————

In Norse mythology, the northern lights appear as Bifröst Bridge, connecting Earth with Asgard, the realm of the gods.

———————

Estonian folklore says that the lights are from a magical carriage taking the gods to a heavenly wedding.

OTHER NATURAL PHENOMENA

Every Irish person knows that leprechauns hide their gold at the end of a rainbow so it will be almost impossible to find.

New Zealand's Te Arawa tribe say the boiling geysers across the North Island are caused by fire demons, summoned many years ago, to save the life of a dying Maori priest.

Madame Pele, the hot-tempered Hawaiian goddess of volcanoes, is not to be crossed—everyone knows when she's angry! Some people still take the precaution of leaving food and flowers for her, just to be on the safe side.

MYTHICAL JOURNEYS

One of the most popular themes in tales, old and new, is a journey. Sometimes they depict the discovery of new lands, creatures, or people. On other occasions, journeys are taken in the spirit of seeking adventure.

Quest stories find the hero searching for something more specific. He or she could have been sent to find a treasure or trophy, to find someone who is lost, or to learn something important that will change his or her life.

JASON AND THE GOLDEN FLEECE

Jason, the rightful king of Thessaly, Greece, is sent on a quest by his usurping uncle Pelias. Pelias challenges Jason to find the legendary golden ram's fleece, which hangs on a branch in an oak grove guarded by fire-breathing bulls and a fearsome dragon. If he succeeds, Pelias will step aside and let Jason reclaim his throne.

Jason sets sail in his ship, the *Argo*, with his men, who become known as the Argonauts. They encounter terrifying storms, clashing rocks, a group of giants with six arms (called the Gegeines), fire-breathing oxen, vicious half-human birds called harpies, a magical army born from dragon's teeth, and even a robot-like creature named Talos!

Each time, thanks to their courage and ingenuity, the heroes succeed, and Jason eventually returns to Thessaly with the fleece to be crowned king. But this is not the end of his adventures, for there are many more legends of Jason, the Argonauts, and their families.

QUEST FOR THE HOLY GRAIL

The Grail is a religious artifact with great powers of regeneration and healing, and it is featured in many quest stories. In Arthurian legend, it was believed to have been kept in a strange castle in the middle of mysterious wastelands, and many of King Arthur's knights set out to search for it.

The vessel could only be found by the purest of heart. Although the knights were brave and bold, most of them were not considered to be worthy. Eventually, the shining knight Sir Galahad passed all the tests—saving Sir Percival from 20 enemies and rescuing many maidens in distress. He had proved himself and was allowed to take the Grail to the isle of Sarras, where it was lifted to heaven, away from human failings.

THE SEVEN STORIES OF SINBAD

One Thousand and One Nights is a series of folktales told around the bazaars of the Middle East for centuries. Often one story starts and leads to a second, which must be told before the first one can continue.

In *Sinbad the Sailor*, a poor porter goes to the house of the rich merchant Sinbad, who tells him the seven stories of how, as a young man, he went to sea to make his fortune.

Each voyage Sinbad takes is more incredible than the last. He encounters monsters, kings, giants, and the terrifying Old Man of the Sea, but also finds amazing lands and wealth beyond his imagination. He is always shipwrecked and often in danger but uses his cunning to save the day.

In the second of the seven stories, a shipwrecked Sinbad ties himself to the talons of a giant bird of prey called a roc in order to escape. The bird unknowingly flies him to its nest in a valley filled with diamonds. Eventually, he is rescued by some merchants, and Sinbad returns home a very rich man indeed!

PANDORA'S BOX:
BE CAREFUL WHAT YOU OPEN

In Greek mythology, the gods were so angry that Prometheus had stolen their fire to give to humans that they decided to punish mankind. Zeus ordered Hephaestus to make the first woman, Pandora, and the gods gave her gifts of beauty, charm, and talent, but also an insatiable curiosity....

Pandora was given a mysterious box, which she was told never to open. Unable to resist a peek inside, she disobeyed, and as she lifted the lid, out flew all the evils of the world. She slammed the box shut immediately, but it was too late. Every evil had escaped. There was just one small quality left at the bottom of the box—hope.

MYTHICAL REALMS

People have always imagined extraordinary places—lost civilizations where huge riches, magic, and beauty await anyone who manages to find them.

In the mountains of South America lies the legend of El Dorado, a shining city that was supposedly made from pure gold. Hundreds of explorers have lost their lives trying to find the city, and it remains lost to this day.

The philosopher Plato famously made up the underwater city of Atlantis, but people still believed it existed. It even appears on some early maps!

Shangri-La is the beautiful but mythical valley where people hardly grow old at all. It first appears in the novel *Lost Horizon,* by James Hilton.

The lost city of gold—
El Dorado

MINI STORIES: MYTHICAL JOURNEYS

Legend tells of two Hungarian princes who chased a strange deer whose antlers glittered with light. They followed the stag to faraway lands before it disappeared into a lake. The brothers built a temple on the land, and they married two local princesses. It is told that their children founded two nations— the Huns and the Magyars.

In Maori legend, Maui-mua searches for his missing sister, Hina-uri. He travels long distances, breaking through the heavens and even turning himself into a bird to find her.

LEGENDARY LOVE STORIES

Everyone enjoys a story of romance, especially if the lovers battle through hardships to be together and emerge triumphant.

One example is the Roman story of Cupid and Psyche. The two lovers become separated after angering Cupid's mother, Venus. Psyche has to undertake many dangerous missions to win back her true love, but eventually she succeeds, and the lovers are reunited forever. We love a happy ending!

LOVE BLOSSOMS

The Hawaiian goddess Pele once saw a handsome human warrior named Ohia, and she fell instantly in love. Unfortunately for Pele, Ohia had already given his heart to Lehua, a local girl. Pele was furious—how dare a mortal turn down a goddess? In anger, she turned Ohia into a twisted, ugly old tree as an act of revenge for rejecting her.

Lehua's heart was broken. The other gods took pity on her, but they could not reverse Pele's powerful magic. Instead, they turned Lehua into a beautiful red flower on Ohia's tree so they could be together forever.

It is said that you should never pick a red lehua blossom, as the sky will fill with the lovers' tears.

LOVE'S LIGHT

The Ramayana is the ancient Indian myth of Prince Rama's search for his lost princess, Sita.

Sita was kidnapped by the evil demon Ravana, who hid her in his secret fortress. Ravana had 10 heads and 20 arms and carried a magic blessing so no human, god, or spirit could kill him.

Rama and his brother Lakshmana go through many adventures together in search of Sita. Finally, they amass an army of monkeys and bears, led by the wise ape Hanuman, who manages to bypass Ravana's magic charm and restore the princess to her prince. Everyone returns home, and India rejoices in an age of plenty.

Even today, people celebrate the triumph of good over evil by lighting candles at the annual festival of light, Diwali.